O9-AIG-416

D0015152

The Woodcutter's Christmas

THE WOODCUTTER'S CHRISTMAS

BRAD KESSLER

PHOTOGRAPHS BY DONA ANN McADAMS

Council Oak Books
San Francisco / Tulsa

A portion of the royalties from the sale of this book are being donated
to an organization benefiting the homeless in New York City.

Council Oak Books, LLC

1290 Chestnut Street, Ste. 2, San Francisco, CA 94109

1350 E. 15th Street, Tulsa, OK 74120

THE WOODCUTTER'S CHRISTMAS.

Copyright © 2001 by Brad Kessler.

Photographs copyright © 2001 by Dona Ann McAdams.

All rights reserved.

Book and jacket design by Melanie Haage.

ISBN 1-57178-105-6

First edition / First printing.

Printed in South Korea.

01 02 03 04 05 06   5 4 3 2 1

EACH YEAR THE WOODCUTTER CAME to our corner. He'd arrive the first of December, like a bird who returned for the wrong season, with his battered truck and his load of Christmas trees. He set up his stock beneath our window, angling fir and spruce trees against a wooden staging. He'd unload a netting barrel, an aluminum lawn chair, a saw, his ax; and afterward, he strung electric lights so they made a kind of arcade over the sidewalk. Overnight the air on First Avenue and Ninth Street became scented with balsam and spruce, so it seemed by the following morning, that a forest had sprung up on our street.

He was a tall man, with whitening hair, sky-blue eyes set deep in their sockets, and a perpetually startled look about him, as if he were always surprised to find himself in the middle of Manhattan and not somewhere out in the woods. To our children, he cut a figure of fascination, in his dove-gray down vest and checkered wool hat and his two-ton Ford rusted to burnt sienna. For three weeks, the Woodcutter perched below our window, sawdust piling around him, his trees dwindling, a transistor radio tuned to some news station. Some nights he stayed on the sidewalk in his lawn chair, and others he slept inside his truck. He never wandered too far from his trees, yet he always vanished the day before Christmas, so by Christmas Eve, on the corner of Ninth Street, there'd be no trace of him. No trees. No radio. Not even a fir needle was left behind.

Sometimes we brought him food: a piece of cake or a sandwich, for he lived those weeks alone, on the street, with no one to care for him and nothing but the corner deli for food. His name, we learned, was simply "Vars" and he came from the Green Mountains of Vermont where he lived alone with his aging mother.

Aside from this, we knew little about the Woodcutter. Ellen and I asked him to our apartment several times, but he always politely refused. One evening, however, there was a problem with his Ford and he buzzed our apartment. He asked through the intercom if we might keep an eye on his trees while he went to a parts store to purchase what he needed. It was around dinnertime and I urged him to come upstairs, that we'd call the auto store from our apartment and watch his trees from the window. He hesitated, then said he didn't want to be a nuisance, but I insisted and pressed the buzzer to let him in.

When the Woodcutter appeared at our apartment, he stood awkwardly in the threshold, shuffling from foot to foot. Philip and Eve rushed to the hall and stood shyly behind their mother—as if Santa himself had come to our door. The Woodcutter smelled of the cold outside, and of unwashed clothes; he held a distributor cap in one hand and his wool hat in the other. Dinner was on the table and Ellen took him gently by the arm, steered him inside and said, "Please stay for supper. I won't take no for an answer. You can wash in the bathroom." He seemed embarrassed by the fuss, but did as she said. I took the distributor cap and called the auto store and arranged to have the replacement delivered to our door. Meanwhile the Woodcutter came back from washing and sat tentatively at the table, unsure how to proceed. He ate sparingly, self-consciously, the children staring at him from behind their plates. Afterward, he laid down his fork, thanked us, and said he had to get back to his trees. He scribbled his address on a scrap of newspaper and apologized for not having a phone, but said we were welcome at his home in the Green Mountains anytime: summer, spring, winter, or fall.

The following December arrived and the Woodcutter didn't show. The second week passed and the sidewalk remained empty, with no alley of trees or smell of spruce, no lawn chair or string of electric lights. The children waited each evening by the window hoping to see his truck. By the second week of December when he still hadn't appeared, we began to worry that something had happened to him. We searched for the scrap of paper with his address. All that was written on it was "Vars" and "Dedham's Notch, Vermont" with no phone number or street address or zip code. The children insisted we write at once, which we did, asking if he was okay. We signed the letter and sent it off directly in the mail.

Two weeks later a plain postal card arrived from Dedham's Notch. The Woodcutter thanked us for our concern and wrote that he couldn't sell his trees in New York City any longer. He invited us again to his home, and wrote that if we visited, perhaps he could explain why.

The children were crestfallen. They wanted to head immediately to Dedham's Notch and find out what had happened. Eve (who still confused the Woodcutter with Santa) thought one of his reindeer had fallen ill and couldn't make the journey. Philip speculated (mischievously) that the Woodcutter had mishandled his chainsaw and had done some irreparable damage to his leg. Whatever the reason, the sidewalk remained empty, unadorned, and the season passed with no Woodcutter and no trees beneath our window. The next year came and once again the Woodcutter didn't show, nor did he appear the year after. Soon he

became merely a memory. Yet as each season approached, the children stared longingly out the window, hoping that that year, he might come back once again.

THREE years after we'd last seen the Woodcutter, we went skiing in Vermont the week before Christmas. Eve was now in third grade and Philip had just entered junior high. We'd finished our vacation and were heading home late one afternoon as the light was fading over the Green Mountains, and a few flakes began to drift over the road. Suddenly from the backseat Eve shouted, "Look! Dedham's Notch." She thrust a hand into the front and pointed toward a sign at the side of the road. Philip tore himself from his book. Ellen glanced over; I saw it too: a black road sign with a white arrow that read "Dedham's Notch: 20 Miles."

"Turn around Dad," Philip yelled. "Turn around!"

"Yeah," Eve shouted, "that's where the Woodcutter lives!"

The sign flew past in the headlights. The children kept shouting to turn around. I thought it a foolish idea given the snow and the hastening hour. Besides, I explained, the Woodcutter would hardly appreciate us descending on him with no warning in the middle of the evening. Yet they wouldn't listen, and to make matters worse, Ellen laid a hand on my wrist. "Come on," she said, "aren't you curious? It's only twenty miles away. We'll just drop in and say hello."

Against my better judgment, I pulled over, backed up, and drove down the exit ramp. The snow was making wet crystals on the windshield now, the road blanketing before us. We crept along a narrow lane, over bridges, along ravines, the forests stretching on either side. The wind lashed snow into our headlights; the night grew dark. The whole time, we saw no other traveler coming in or out of that country.

Just as we were abandoning hope of ever reaching Dedham's Notch, we came upon a church under a dawn-to-dusk light, and a cluster of houses capped with snow, and a sign with the name "Vars" painted on it. We pulled into his drive and followed a steep track. The car fishtailed in the snow, crested a rise, and at the bottom of a hill we saw a farmhouse with the windows all lit and smoke chuffing from a chimney. The children were unusually quiet, staring at the scene, for the house seemed somehow unreal, like a diorama in a snow dome, with the lights all shining and the snow shedding down around it. And then as if he'd known we were there all along, the Woodcutter appeared in our headlights wearing his checkered wool hat. He didn't seem at all surprised to see us. I rolled down the window. He said

nothing for some time but stood staring in at us, grinning from ear to ear.

His house was warm inside; the smell of woodsmoke greeted us, and a black dog tunneled between our legs. A woman with raven hair and a crooked smile emerged in the hallway, wiped her hands on an apron and said hello. She clearly wasn't old enough to be the Woodcutter's mother. Perhaps she was his sister (though he'd never mentioned any siblings before). She just smiled and nodded at us, and the Woodcutter, realizing our confusion, apologized.

"This is Claire," he explained. "She's . . . my wife."

He blushed then as if he'd spoken some secret. Claire held out a bony hand and smiled gracefully. He'd never mentioned a wife before, but then we hadn't seen him for years and knew little about him in the first place. By now it was obvious to us all that there'd be no further travel that night, for the snow was falling in sheets and the roads would be impassable. The Woodcutter showed us to our rooms. In the kitchen, Claire put out plates of cold turkey, white bread and a jar of mayonnaise. Before we turned upstairs, Eve looked up from her plate and asked the Woodcutter why he didn't come to the city anymore. The Woodcutter merely smiled. "It's late now," he said and patted her on the shoulder. "Tomorrow I'll tell you the whole story."

IN THE MORNING, DEDHAM'S NOTCH lay buried beneath a foot of fresh snow. The children had woken early and were already outside making forts in the yard, the dog leaping around them. Claire had breakfast on the table: stacks of pancakes, sausages, a jar of maple syrup tapped from their own trees.

After breakfast, the Woodcutter took us on a tour of his woodlot. The day was overcast, the clouds feathering down from the mountains. He walked us along an old logging road, through a forest of paper birch and into a field of young spruce trees. The trees stood shoulder high, slate blue, capped with crowns of snow, a field of them stretching up to a plateau where they ended abruptly in a granite cliff he called the Notch.

"Here," he waved his hand over the expanse of trees. "This is where your trees once came from."

He stood a moment in silence, his breath making clouds in the cold. He'd farmed this high plateau for years, he said, cutting the older

growth and planting new saplings each spring. In summer he saw juncos and gray jays and spruce grouse, and in winter there were snowshoe hare and deer, and occasionally a moose, browsing through the branches. The trees liked the altitude there, he said, the soil, the hard winter freezes, which were good for their health.

He plucked three small needles from one of the branches, placed one in his mouth and handed the rest to the children.

"Taste," he said.

Philip put the needle tentatively in his mouth.

"They're full of vitamins," he explained. "The Indians once brewed tea from the needles and in Europe they carved violins from the wood."

A hawk flew overhead and perched in a nearby tree, knocking snow to the ground.

"Red-tailed," he explained to the children, without even looking.

The wind picked up. Some clouds lowered from the Notch. A crow cawed somewhere in the woods, and the hawk flew off. The Woodcutter spat out the needle and said, "Come, I want to show you something."

We followed him to a ring of trees. Philip parted the branches and asked what was inside.

"They're my folks," he nodded. "Take a look."

Philip pushed more branches aside, and we could see within the circle two marble headstones, one more weathered than the other, with no words written on either, and no dates. On top of the newer one stood a Christmas ornament, a tin angel with a trumpet, half hidden in the snow.

By the time we'd walked his whole property and made it back to the house, it was late afternoon and a fire was crackling in the hearth. Claire sat in a rocker in the corner with some knitting. She'd put sandwiches out for the kids. The Woodcutter announced that now he could tell us why he'd stopped coming to Manhattan. We found a place on the couch, the children on the floor beside the fire. The Woodcutter checked the logs, then settled himself heavily into his armchair and looked into the flame.

"As far back as I can remember," he began, "I cut trees—just as my father had, and his father, and his father before him."

He sighed and shifted in the chair and looked at the children once more. Then, as if remembering something, he went on.

"When I was boy no bigger than yourself," he pointed to Philip, "we harvested the hardwoods in the valley. Oaks and ash and maples.

Birches too. We used crosscut saws, the two-man ones, and my father taught me how to set the teeth of a saw close for hardwood, far for soft, and how to wrap my arms 'round a tree and shut my eyes and feel which way she was leaning. When all was quiet and you could feel the tree against your chest, it would tell you where it wanted to fall. That way, we could drop a hundred-foot oak on the head of dime, and we never missed our mark once.

"My earliest memory is of watching trees fall. I saw them during the day, and dreamt of them at night. A puff of air always rose from the place where they crashed. In summer it was dust, and in winter snow, but at all times there was a kind of light that jumped when the tree came down. Woodcutters know about that light. Mother said it was the soul of the tree rising from the earth. She said it was the tree's spirit flying off like an angel, and though I didn't believe her then, I did many years later on.

"Well, we cut up and down the valley, and then came the buzz saws out of Oregon, and they felled a forest as fast as a whole crew once could. Even we were surprised how fast the woods went down, how quick the valley came to meadow, and how much less lumberin' there was around.

"So it was my mother's idea, the Christmas trees. Growing instead of cutting, and not having to find someone else's woodlot to work. It was slow going at first, hauling hundreds of seedlings at a time, digging the holes, feeding and watering them. The first summer we planted more than five hundred trees and the next twice as many, and there was always the upkeep and mulching and clearing brush. I'd watch those saplings grow year to year, putting out new shoots, the sap sweating out like syrup, growing so slowly you'd think they'd never ready themselves for the harvest. It took four years before we cut our first Christmas tree. In another two years' time, we had enough to haul to Manhattan.

"These were fine times, with the trees all grown and full of limbs. Seems as though we always left in the middle of the night, three or four on a cold December morning with the smell of coffee in the cab, and father driving, and the trees all wrapped in netting and piled in the back by size. I was always too excited to sleep, so I'd watch the land pass outside the windows and the day grow bright. By afternoon, we'd reach the outskirts of New York City and cross the East River. We'd drive down Second Avenue through all those cars and trucks into the thick of the city; and I was proud then, with our truck all piled high with trees and us in traffic and people staring from the sidewalk. It was like they'd been waiting for us to arrive, that without our trees they'd have no presents. No Christmas. It made you feel special. It made you feel almost like Santa.

"Now I'd never been far outside the Notch before, so for me arriving in Manhattan was like coming to some strange circus. I'd wander the city when I could, which wasn't too often, since I had to tend the trees. We'd spend two or three weeks on the street, one of us sleeping in the cab while the other watched the stock. Each year, whether we sold all the trees or not, we packed up and headed home in time for Christmas Eve. This was a rule, something sacred. We always had to get back for dinner on Christmas Eve. It wouldn't have been right otherwise, leaving Mother alone.

"Well, the years flew by like this. We broke new fields, increased the acres, tried out new trees. Douglas and Frazer fir. Scotch pine. Colorado blues. We made enough from the trees to get by, what with the sugarin' and a little lumberin' on the side. It was rough work, and Father was growing older all the time. One afternoon in October when the leaves were in full color, he fell while planting some trees. It was one of those bright autumn days when the wind was a knife out of the Notch. I found him hours later, near suppertime, down on his hands and knees, hair in his face, unable to stand up. I had to carry him home to the house. The doctor in Rutland said it was the cancer, that his body was filled with it. We brought him home and set him in a chair beside the window, but he didn't want to talk about any of it. A month later, on the new moon, he died.

"After that, things changed around the house. I worked double-hard just to keep the place up and get the trees all cut in time. Mother tried the best she could, and I headed to the city alone, driving all night and setting up the trees, then rushing back three weeks later in time for Christmas dinner, as Mother would be waiting. It was a lonely business, and it went like that for many years, twenty or so. I couldn't even count them, as there was hardly time to stop. I didn't notice how time kept slipping by, and how many trees came in and out of that field, only that by then, those saplings seemed a part of me, the planting and harvesting, the pitch and bark, as if sap itself was the blood that beat in my veins, and my arms were girded 'round with fifty rings of phloem, a new one put on each year that passed. Mother helped when she could, which wasn't very often, with her getting on in the years. I hardly noticed how aged she'd become, until she too took sick with a stroke, and then died three years ago. It was August then; we'd been having a heat wave. She was eighty-nine years by my reckoning. It happened so sudden, and then I was left alone, overnight, in the house, with not even a dog or a cat for comfort.

"I buried her out in the field where the spruces grow, back where we'd put Father in the ground. I set a dozen saplings 'round their stones as a kind of commemoration. I remember coming off the hill that afternoon after the saplings were in, my hands covered with mud, and the house so quiet I didn't know what to do. I sat in the kitchen for a long time not washing, just wondering how I'd get on and what I'd do all by myself. The wind kept blowing pine needles through the backdoor. Then it began to rain and I sat right there with the door open and the evening coming on and the smell of rain on the roof. I fell asleep at the table while the wind banged the shutters and the needles grew wet on the floor. And I stayed there the next day too, not knowing what to do. I think it took two days before I had the strength to rise again and wash that mud off my hands."

The Woodcutter paused. He grabbed a poker from the wall and leaned forward and sifted the embers in the hearth, then sank back in his chair.

"Well," he sighed, "that was a hard autumn for sure, with the house so quiet like I'd never known it, and the only sound the wind rushing in the trees outside, so it seemed at times as if someone were whispering my name. I never thought of myself as alone before up here on the Notch, and I'd never thought myself old either, because mother was always around. But that autumn everything changed and I felt all at once different, both old and all alone.

"When December came, I cut the load of Christmas trees and made the journey to the city as before. I set up my trees in the same spot.

Only things that year were not the same at all. No one was waiting for me back home in Dedham's Notch, and I had no reason to return so quickly before Christmas. So when Christmas Eve came, I didn't rush home as always, but decided to stay in the city. What did I have to lose? I'd find a hotel room and stay for a day or two. Maybe take in the sights, walk the streets like I did when I was a boy. Maybe things wouldn't be so bad after all.

"Christmas Day I parked the truck in a lot and checked into a cheap hotel off Second Avenue. I slept most of that first day, for it was the first warm bed I'd been in for weeks. The next morning, I set off to explore, but before I got too far I saw one of my own trees lying on the sidewalk. I recognized it immediately. I'd been around those trees long enough that I could tell them apart from others, just as you can pick a familiar face from a crowd of a hundred. It's the same with those trees, for each have their own look and odor and way of growing, and I can pick a needle from a tree and tell from its taste if its roots are rotten or diseased, or if it needs more acid or lime.

"So when I saw my own tree lying on the sidewalk that day, it was like coming across my own kin. Seeing it in that strange place shocked me a little. I wondered if something was wrong with it, as it was only the day after Christmas and somebody had already thrown it away. I knelt down and checked the trunk for rot or beetles or excess sap. I stood it upright. People were passing on the sidewalk, looking at me, then looking at the tree. It was a black spruce the size of a child, perfectly healthy, with ten rings around its heart. I couldn't see leaving it out there alone, so I slung it over my shoulder and carried it back to the hotel where I found a bowl of water for it and stood it beside my bed.

"When I went out again later, it was snowing and I saw another tree, and then another, each discarded on the sidewalk. By the afternoon, I began keeping count. I walked up Second Avenue, and before I'd made it to Forty-second Street, I'd counted over fifty trees. Some were wrapped in plastic, others bound with rope; some stuffed into trash cans; others just lay on the curb with no covering at all. I hadn't realized how many trees traveled to New York City each December, and how quickly they were cast away, so soon after Christmas. It was strange. I felt somehow cheated, seeing them all in the gutter, dying by the hundreds, as if the toil of all my year had come to this, had been discarded in a single day.

"That evening back at the hotel, I couldn't help thinking about the trees. I'd never given much thought to what happened to them after Christmas. I always imagined them in homes with ornaments on them and glass bulbs and boxes beneath the branches. I'd seen Christmas

trees thrown away in Dedham's Notch, but never in such numbers or so soon after the holiday, and it struck me then, with all those trees scattered on the sidewalk, what a great waste it was, that it was somehow wrong; that if the trees were abandoned so quickly, so unceremoniously, what was the point of ever having one in the first place? I thought about every tree I'd ever cut and carried and sold in New York City and I calculated over six thousand trees in all. Six thousand, maybe even more, thrown on the sidewalk right after Christmas Day.

"I couldn't sleep that night. Midnight came and I lay awake. The radiators hissed in the room; a siren went up the avenue. At three in the morning, I began to hear something strange. As the streets grew quiet, I heard wind blowing in tree branches. I thought I was imagining it at first, because there were no trees in the middle of Manhattan. But the longer I lay in bed, the louder the sound became. It was peaceful at first, like branches bending in a high wind, but then the sound turned into a vibration, a scratching noise, like fingernails scraping down a blackboard. And beneath it all, I heard voices inside that wind whispering, murmuring, speaking to me. It was the trees talking; I was convinced of it! They wanted to be taken away, off the streets, and brought back to the mountains. They wanted to get back inside the earth. They were crying out to be saved.

"I shot up in bed, unsure if I was dreaming. I shut my eyes and heard the voices again, distinct, horrible, like a chorus in my head, a choir of a hundred souls caught in some awful anguish, scratching, scraping, *speaking only to me.* I thought, my God, I am surely going mad.

"So I made a promise to myself, a kind of pact, sitting there in the dark. I promised to take all the abandoned trees I could off the streets, to bring them back to the mountains for a proper burial among the spruce grouse and gray jays, because they were like a family to me, the only real family I had. For this, all I wanted was to stop hearing the scratching in my head. All I wanted was my sanity, and I'd head back home and never sell another tree in Manhattan again.

"I fell asleep sometime early that morning. I dreamt of my mother and father, of the field of spruce trees. I dreamt the discarded trees were trudging up a hill. When I woke, the roar of traffic startled me. I'd forgotten where I was. The day was bright in the window, the streets already busy below. I dressed quickly and went downstairs, paid my bill and hurried out to the truck. The voices were gone from my head now, but I was convinced I'd heard them. So when I spotted the first abandoned tree, I leapt out of the cab and retrieved it, just as I'd vowed. I drove west along the street, searching for trees. Every time I saw one, I pulled over and pitched it in the back of the truckbed. People were

shouting at me, honking their horns, but I didn't care. I found all manner of trees: spruce, pine, fir, one burnt and blackened, another shoved between two telephone booths. Some lay in the gutter, others were tossed away on top of dumpsters.

"I collected them for hours, and by afternoon, the truck was filled to the slats. I was somewhere near Tenth Avenue by then and I pulled into a parking space and found one last tree wrapped in a canvas tarp. I heaved it on top of the others and started back to the cab, when a voice stopped me from behind.

"'You're from the Green Mountains,' someone said.

"I turned and saw a woman bundled in a large black overcoat. She wore a red beret and a yellow scarf wrapped around her neck several times. I must have looked startled, because she stepped back and pointed to the rear of the truck.

"'I saw your license plate,' she said.

"'Oh,' I nodded.

"She pulled her scarf down and exposed her mouth. Her skin was pale and looked red and cracked from the cold. She had a gray rucksack on her back and plastic bags in her boots. I realized she was a street woman, homeless probably, perhaps a panhandler. She was staring at the trees in the back of my truck.

"'I was once in those mountains,' she said, 'but that was a long time ago.' She turned to me and bit the inside of her mouth. 'You're a lucky man for living there.'

"'Yes,' I nodded, 'I suppose I am.'

"She was silent a moment, looking again at the truck. I wished her a good afternoon and turned to go, yet she stopped me.

"'Wait,' she said. 'What are you doing with those trees?'

"'Picking them up,' I told her.

"She smiled and said she knew that, but *why* was I doing it? I didn't want to tell her the real reason, because I wasn't sure myself and it would've sounded too crazy besides. But then I looked at her overcoat and the filthy beret, and I figured she was probably mad herself, so what did I care what she thought?

"'I'm taking them back to Vermont,' I explained. 'They deserve better than to be thrown out a day after Christmas. I'm taking them back to where they belong to let them die peacefully.'

"She looked at me oddly a moment. It seemed I'd said something deeply wounding. A wind blew up the street and she pulled the scarf tighter to her neck.

"'It's a good thing you're doing,' she finally said. 'All things need a burial, a place to go to.' She shook her head, then fixed me with two brown eyes. 'I used to have a place to go to,' she explained, 'but that was a long time ago.'

"I asked her where she lived now and she grinned and swept a hand at the buildings and said, 'Here, in New York City, the Greatest City on Earth.' She chuckled, lowered her eyes to the sidewalk and forced a smile. 'Life's like that,' she said. 'One day you're the center of the universe with a star overhead, and the next you're on the street.'

"I didn't know what to say. I had the sudden impulse to tell her about my mother's death. Some people were passing on the sidewalk, moving wide to avoid us. I told her it was nice to have met her, but I best be getting on, that it was a long journey back north and I wanted to make it before midnight.

"'Are you taking more trees?' she asked.

"I looked at the truck; the bed was filled to the top.

"'I've taken enough,' I said.

"She nodded and mumbled something, pulling her beret down over her ears. I noticed then that her teeth were chattering. The poor woman, I thought, alone after Christmas, out on the streets with nowhere to go. The least I could do was offer her some money. I felt I should do something good, a kind of penance, especially after the night I'd just had. So I dug in my pockets for change, but didn't want to insult her. There was, across the avenue, a coffee shop with its lights on. I stuffed my hands in my pockets and nodded across the street.

"'It's cold out here,' I said. 'Would you want a cup of soup or something?'

"'Soup?' she asked.

"'Yes,' I said, 'or a coffee.'

"She bit her lip as if I'd said something funny. I could see the bones of her cheeks, so skinny she was, like a skeleton, with her two big eyes staring into space. She muttered something again and giggled and I was sure she was mad, so I turned to leave.

"'Sorry,' she stopped me. 'It's just . . . well.' She swept her scarf back and looked at her hand. 'It's just been a while since someone's asked me . . . to soup.'

"I said if she didn't want to, it was fine with me.

"'No, no, I'd love to,' she said.

"So we started across the street together. A strange lot we must have looked. Me unshaven and covered in pine needles and sap, and she in her filthy getup and rucksack and the plastic bags in her boots.

"We found two stools at the end of the counter. She fished inside a pocket and pulled out a crumpled pack of Pall Malls and tried to

light one. Her matches were damp, and after a while she gave up and dropped it in an ashtray.

"The coffee came and we sat over our mugs not speaking. I ordered some doughnuts, a chocolate and a coconut and two with colored sprinkles, and she broke the coconut into little pieces and ate each one delicately as if they were some kind of fine food.

"After she finished the doughnut and the waitress refilled her mug, she began to tell me how she came to New York at the age of nineteen from a small town in North Carolina. She was a dancer, she said, who'd danced in musicals on Broadway, and at Radio City Music Hall. She talked about her boyfriends, and then her marriage to an advertising man. She spoke about their high life together, the parties, the drinking, and how her life had taken a turn for the worse. She spoke about being careless and something about drugs and ending up in a hospital, and how she'd never be able to dance again. Then her husband had left her, had taken everything, and she'd lost her apartment, her job. The rest I couldn't quite understand, only that she'd been living on and off in a shelter for the past year and was trapped in a city she never thought was home.

"She lifted her mug and sipped. She grabbed the cigarette from the ashtray and finally succeeded in lighting it. Her hands were trembling, the cigarette shaking. I didn't know what to say. I felt I'd gotten in over my head and suddenly wanted to leave. I didn't even know if any of what she said was true, the music hall, the advertising man, the hospital. She looked up as if she'd read my mind and mashed the cigarette in the ashtray and dabbed her mouth with the napkin in a ladylike way. And I felt bad then that I'd doubted her, for there was something delicate, almost graceful about her, even in that state, beneath the beret and the bad skin. I thought to myself, perhaps she is telling the truth.

"The waitress came by and left the bill on the counter. I told the woman I'd be right back and headed to the men's room. Inside the stall, I counted two hundred dollars from the tree money and rolled the bills into a bundle. That would be enough for a few good meals at least, maybe enough for a place to stay a couple of nights. It was something, at any rate. I walked out of the bathroom back to our seats, yet when I reached them, she was gone. Her stool was empty; she was nowhere in sight. The waitress, who was wiping the counter nearby, jerked a thumb toward the door.

"'She left,' she said, 'while you were in the bathroom. She took off.'

"I was, at once, relieved. I shoved the dollars deeper in my pocket. Perhaps the woman *was* crazy after all; perhaps her story was all lies.

Perhaps she was just a homeless woman hustling a cup of coffee. The waitress shrugged and I thanked her, then I went to pay the bill.

"Outside, darkness was falling, the streetlights buzzing. The wind felt raw on my cheek. I hurried back to the truck. The woman was nowhere in sight. I was eager to get out of that place, even though I'd be returning to the empty house. Anything seemed better than the last forty-eight hours, with the voices in my head, the dead Christmas trees scattered on the sidewalks and then the homeless woman disappearing from the coffee shop. I climbed into the cab and breathed a sigh of relief as I turned the engine and headed north for home."

THE Woodcutter paused. The fire had burned low. He rose and maneuvered another log onto the hearth and positioned it with a poker. The children watched with their heads cradled on their knees. Then the Woodcutter returned to his seat once more, laced his fingers together, and sighed.

"Well," he began, "it was good to get away from those streets. Away from all that noise and light. Just me and my truck loaded down with trees traveling north. The highways were salted, the lanes all empty. The darkness came quick. I drove through the night. The farther

north I drove, the more my thoughts turned to home and the years before, how Mother would always be waiting for me with a meal keeping warm on the stove and the lights burning in the house, and how we'd sit and talk for hours about what had happened in Manhattan and how good it was to be home. But that year, I knew I'd be coming home to a cold house, with the furnace shut down and the pipes all drained. And there'd be no one waiting for me, no one to tell about the dead trees and the voices and the street woman. And a new fear crept into my bones, for I was afraid I'd hear the voices again, the ones I'd heard in the hotel. I was afraid they'd follow me all the way back to Dedham's Notch.

"I made it home around midnight. The house was cold as iron, the windows etched with rime. I switched on the furnace and built a fire in the hearth and turned the water taps on. I still kept expecting Mother there, in the kitchen or in her room. A sadness swept over me as I imagined the long winter ahead with little left for me to do.

"I climbed the staircase and slipped into my freezing bed. I was so tired from the drive and all that had happened in the city, I fell instantly asleep. Yet sometime later I awoke to a sound. I couldn't tell if I'd been dreaming. The moon was in the window, then I heard it again, a kind of boom, like a door closing. I climbed from bed and crept to the head of the stairs and listened. I heard only the sound of the wind outside and the furnace firing in the cellar, and the squeak of a flying squirrel in the wall. So I went back to bed, and thought I was just hearing things again. I stayed awake for a long time listening to my heart like the beating of a hammer on a box, until finally I was overcome with sleep."

"The next morning I woke rested. The voices were gone, the strange sounds too. I made a big breakfast in the kitchen. I was beginning to think that maybe things would be okay, when I went outside afterwards to the truck. It was a gray day with a dusting of fresh snow on the ground. Down by the truck, I saw footprints in the snow. Then I remembered the sound in the night, and my heart began to race again, for it seemed some intruder had come in the dark. I stepped closer to the truck and saw a dozen footprints going one way and the other. What I saw next startled me even more: half the trees were missing from the bed of the truck!

"I stood for a moment in utter confusion. I almost believed the trees had sprouted legs and walked away on their own accord! Just as I'd heard them crying in the night, just as I dreamt about them, they'd picked up on their own and walked away. I could even see the path of the footprints, leading up the old logging road behind the house. But it was impossible. Surely, I thought, I was seeing things!

"I closed my eyes. I tried to keep calm. Either someone had come in the night, I reasoned, or I was truly going mad. I did the only thing that seemed to make sense at the time. I hurried back in the house and grabbed the Springfield from my closet. Whatever was out there, intruder or not, I wanted to be prepared for it. I loaded the magazine and stuffed a few shells in my pocket. Then I went outside again and followed the trail of footprints. They led up the logging road, up to the plateau of spruces, out into the field where I'd been planting the trees for years.

"On the far side of the field I spied something moving. I levered the rifle and chambered a round, raised the rifle and peered through the scope. Two legs were walking beneath a tree. I didn't know if it was human or phantom or what kind of unearthly creature it was, but I kept moving toward it, steadily, hiding behind the saplings, going from one tree to the next.

"When I was close enough, I stepped out in the open and shouted, 'Who are you?'

"The tree stopped in its tracks.

"'Who are you?' I shouted again, louder, my fingers trembling on the trigger.

"The figure turned and dropped the tree and I saw it was the street woman with the red beret and the yellow scarf, looking as surprised as myself. She shrieked when she saw the gun, and dropped to the ground. Yet my mind couldn't put the pieces together, how she could be in New York City one moment and here in my field the next.

"'What are you doing here?' I shouted, the blood beating hard in my head. She was screaming now hysterically, her hands covering her face, pleading for me to put the gun down.

"I lowered the rifle, and she put a hand to her chest and closed her eyes. I waited for her to speak; she still seemed a sort of phantom to me. Then slowly, she rose and brushed pine needles from her coat, and we stood staring at each other a moment. She was covered in dried needles and panting in the cold. I could see her lips had a bluish tint about them and she was shivering—from fright or the cold, I couldn't tell.

"'What are you doing here?' I asked.

"'I'm sorry,' she swallowed. 'You said the trees needed to come back here. I just . . . wanted to help.'

"'You wanted to help?'

"'Yes,' she nodded. 'I hid in the truck . . . in the back. When you went to the bathroom, I slipped away. I didn't mean any harm. I only wanted to bring the trees here. I just wanted . . . I just . . . ' She was shaking now, her shoulders slumped. There were tears welling in her eyes. 'I had nowhere to go,' she said and began sobbing in earnest.

"I didn't know what to say. I thought for certain she was out of her mind, for what kind of person would jump into the back of a stranger's truck and ride five hours in the cold? I thought maybe she was unreal, that I'd made her up, just like the voices in the night. I closed my eyes and opened them. A wind cut across the field and she clutched her coat tighter to her neck.

"'You hid in the truck,' I asked, 'the whole time?'

"She looked up shyly like a girl who'd done something wrong. 'I found a blanket,' she said.

"'A blanket?'

"'Yes,' she nodded and ran the back of her hand across her nose. 'It wasn't that bad.'

"I shook my head and stood the rifle at my side. I was completely dumbfounded. I had no idea what to do with her. I could see that crystals had formed on the tips of her eyelashes.

"'You'll catch your death out here,' I said, 'if you haven't already from the ride. Let's get in out of the cold.'

"She looked at the tree that she'd just dropped on the ground.

"'What about the trees?' she asked.

"'What about them?'

"'They're still in the truck.'

"'They'll be fine,' I said.

"She hesitated and glanced again at the tree on the ground and pointed to its top limb. 'There's an ornament on that one,' she said. 'Someone left it on the branch.'

"'That's okay,' I said impatiently. 'Let's get back to the house'

"'But look,' she insisted, pointing at the ornament on the tree. 'It's a tin angel.'

"I waved a hand and said I didn't care if it was the devil himself, that she needed to get inside before she froze herself to death.

"We started back through the snow. I followed behind, keeping an eye on her. My mind was all jumbled and confused. She began talking quickly, girlishly, about the snow and the mountains, how beautiful they were, and how long she'd been in the city that she'd forgotten places like this actually existed. She commented on everything, the rabbit tracks, the chickadees, the sound of a birch creaking in the wind. She smiled and I thought again that she was out of her mind, that the safest thing to do was to put her on a bus back to New York City as fast as I could manage.

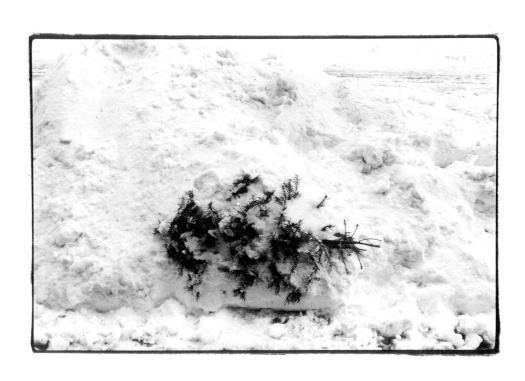

"We reached the house. I leaned the rifle against the wall, but saw her look at it, and I picked it up again. In the kitchen, I turned the stove on high and sat her near it to warm. Her lips were still trembling. I found a quilt for her to wrap herself in. I asked if she wanted something hot to eat, and she said, yes she wouldn't mind.

"I opened a can of tomato soup and stuck it on the stove and toasted two slices of bread. She was looking around at the kitchen with a strange unearthly smile, a kind of grin that was frightening. The minute after she finished her soup, I thought, I'd take her to the bus station in Rutland.

"When the soup was hot, I placed a bowl before her. She'd taken off her beret by now and her hair was loose in her face. She was upset at first that I wasn't eating, but then she ate quickly, hungrily, wolfing down the bread, spooning soup into her mouth and wiping tomato from her chin from time to time. I had no appetite myself; I was preparing to tell her she had to leave, that I'd drive her to Rutland where she could catch a bus back to Manhattan. She looked up from her bowl then and fixed me in her gaze.

"'Your mother died last summer, didn't she?' she said.

"'How do you know that?' I asked.

"'You told me in New York,' she said.

"I didn't remember telling her any such thing.

"'It must be lonely,' she said, 'being up here all alone.'

"'You get used to it,' I said.

"She put her spoon down and stared at me hard with her brown eyes. 'No,' she said. 'You never get used to being alone.'

"She picked up her empty bowl and plate and walked to the sink. I tried to stop her, but she ignored me. She took the pot from the stove too and grabbed an apron from a peg beside the sink and tied it to her waist. I began to tell her to take it off, for it was Mother's apron, but it was already too late. She had started washing dishes like she owned the place. I slid back in my chair. I felt suddenly weary and deflated. The water was running, the windows steaming. Her back was turned to me and then I heard her voice.

"'I could help you know,' she said, 'around here.'

"'Help?' I asked.

"'With the house,' she said. 'I used to keep a good house. I could do it again.'

"I sat at the table and said nothing. I'd have no mad women working for me. No, I thought, best to get rid of her as quick as I could. But I felt suddenly weary again, helpless in my own house, with this strange street woman doing my dishes as if she were some enchantress who'd come into my home and cast a spell of sleep over me, as if everything that had happened in the last two days had been the result of some strange charm, first the trees crying in the night, then the footprints, and now this. I could hardly keep open my eyes.

"I checked the Springfield leaning against the wall; it was still within reach. Then I looked again at the woman. She was still at the sink washing dishes, her back to me. Her sweater had holes along the elbows. Her hair was unwashed and streaked with gray, held in the back with a red rubber band. Perhaps she was just a poor woman down on her luck after all, I thought, not dangerous, but just desperate enough to take a fool's chance in a stranger's truck.

"A wave of exhaustion washed over me. I felt almost dizzy, with the sound of that sink water, and a cloud of steam rising from where she stood. I wondered about the bus schedule, what time we'd have to get to Rutland. I told her I had to go upstairs a moment, that I'd be right back. I didn't know what was happening; it felt like I was suffocating. She didn't turn around once. I left the kitchen and staggered upstairs. When I reached my room I closed the door and sat on the edge of the bed. I was trying to sort out the events of the last two days, but they were suddenly a blur. I fell back onto the bed and fell at once asleep.

"When I woke, evening was coming on and the sky was purple out the window. It seemed I'd risen from a long sleep, with the deepest dreams I'd ever dreamt. Downstairs, the woman was asleep on the couch, curled up with the old quilt. I left her there, not wanting to wake her, and slipped out the front door.

"Dusk was falling outside. The truck was there, though the trees were all gone now from its bed. I walked into the woods. I needed to get some air, to think. The evening was bracing. I walked for a long time. I went up toward the Notch and down into the woods again. Crows were cawing in the dusk. I didn't have any direction in particular, but I found myself in the field of spruce trees, beside the ring of trees around my mother and father's stones.

"Twilight had come, and the last streaks of red were turning over the forest, the sky a dark velvet above. I parted the branches and peered into the circle. There was my mother's stone and there my father's, side by side, one more worn than the other. I noticed something sparkle on my mother's. I thought it was the light or the glow off the snow or something in my eye. But then I saw it was a Christmas ornament, the tin angel the woman had found earlier on the tree. She must have brought it up there along with the rest of the trees while I was asleep. I picked it up and drew it near. It was very old, an heirloom someone

had mistakenly left on the branches when they threw away the tree. Its wings were painted gold and the paint had chipped in places and its trumpet was beginning to rust. Yet you could see that it was once a pretty thing, a thing someone had cherished. I wiped it against my jacket and looked at the angel again and decided to keep it after all."

LOG SNAPPED IN THE HEARTH and the Woodcutter shifted in his chair.

"Well," he said. "You probably figured by now, I never did ask that street woman to leave. She made a home for herself here, and then she made one for me as well."

He looked across at Claire who was still knitting, and she glanced up at him and blushed. The Woodcutter did too, as if embarrassed by their story. "So that's the reason I don't come to New York City anymore. I have no need for it. Someone else can cut Christmas trees. I just plant them now, each year. Besides, the city is too dangerous for a man who talks to trees."

"And for one who talks to strange women," Claire said, peeking up from her work.

The Woodcutter chuckled and checked his wristwatch. It was dark now outside the windows. The evening had come early and we could see snowflakes falling past the lighted panes. The Woodcutter gripped the sides of his chair and stood.

"Come," he said and gestured for us all to follow. "I want to show you something." He shuffled across the room toward the front door, and we followed, with Claire and the dog behind.

Outside, the night was bracing. Snow was driving down from Canada, angling in the branches and catching in the crowns of the trees and drifting heavily over all the Green Mountains. The Woodcutter was standing on the edge of the porch, alert and listening. He was smiling.

"Hear that?" he said. "They are happy."

We listened. The wind was tunneling through trees. We heard nothing at first, and then slowly it came to us. Behind the house, up on the high plateau, a low moan, a kind of hum, something sleeving in the boreal spruces. The sound grew louder, to a high pitch, as if a bow had been brought against strings, and the trees were resonating together, a chord of wind in the woods. It grew louder and louder and each of us looked at one another with surprise and joy. And then, just as quickly, it quieted again, and the sound ceased altogether and the snow fell as it had before, silently around the house.

ACKNOWLEDGMENTS

I'd like to thank Lori E. Seid and Mark Russell, and the original woodcutter, Patrick J. Fehilly.

Dona Ann McAdams